T*A*C*K
into Danger

created by MARVIN MILLER
written by NANCY K. ROBINSON

illustrated by Alan Tiegreen
cover by Dick Williams

SCHOLASTIC INC.
NEW YORK · TORONTO · LONDON · AUCKLAND · SYDNEY

*For my wonderful parents,
Esther and David Miller.
M.M.*

*To my friends—the talented Teya
and marvelous Marta!
N.K.R.*

ISBN 0-590-33667-3

Reading level is determined by using the Spache Readability Formula.
3.1 signifies average 3rd grade.

Text copyright © 1983 by Marvin Miller and Nancy K. Robinson.
Illustrations copyright © 1983 by Scholastic Inc. All rights reserved.
Published by Scholastic Inc.

12 11 10 9 8 7 6 5 4 3   7 8 9/8 0/9

Printed in U.S.A.   11

CONTENTS

CONTENTS

SANDY HARBOR, SATURDAY, NOVEMBER 1 —

It has been an interesting year for the T*A*C*K team. T*A*C*K, by the way, is an informal network of kids — four kids to be exact — who solve mysteries, everyday problems, and matters of life and death in the small seacoast town of Sandy Harbor. The most important thing about T*A*C*K is the way we work. When everyone else is mystified, when everyone else has given up, the T*A*C*K team steps in.

All four of us lead private lives disguised as ordinary elementary school kids. The word T*A*C*K stands for the first letter of each of our names:

T* is for me, Toria Gardner, the reporter of these events.

A* is for Abigail Pinkwater, my best friend.
   Abby moved to another town. She now lives three hundred miles away in a town called Pleasantville, but she is still a member of T*A*C*K. We call her our Agent-on-Remote.

C* is for Chuck, a tried-and-true member of the team.
   Chuck is well organized and honest, with a good sense of humor, as you will see.

K* is the code name for Will Roberts.
   We stole Will's code name from early telegraph language. Over the wire "K" sounds like this: *dah dih dah* (long short long). It means "SWITCH TO SEND" or "GO AHEAD WITH YOUR MESSAGE." "K" is the perfect code name for Will. His mind switches all over the place. It is our secret weapon.

   Will Roberts hardly ever sees just one answer to a problem. Let me give you an example:
   One day Will and I were in the middle of a chess game when Will suddenly said, "How many

squares do you see on this board, Toria?"

"We can count them later," I said, and I moved my queen right across the board.

"Count them now," Will said.

I counted the squares. "Sixty-four, Will," I answered. "Why do you ask?"

"Wrong," Will said. "There are many more than that. Sixty-four plus . . ."

Will counted blocks of four squares — each block makes one bigger square. Then he counted blocks of nine squares (three across and three down), and so on. "And, of course, there's the square formed by the whole chessboard . . ."

"Very clever, Will," I said. "Do you mind if we finish this game? Your king is in check. If you don't watch out, I'm going to take it."

Will went on to win the game — I was so tired from all that counting.

It's silly to go into too much detail about T*A*C*K right at this minute. Just let me add that my real name is Victoria Gardner; I want to be a foreign correspondent when I grow up and sail around the world in my own sailboat covering big news stories; and, finally, I have a little sister named Holly.

Let me start by telling you what happened on the 14th of June . . .

The Comic Book Caper

"I need a comic book," my little sister Holly said.

Will and I were standing outside Beebee's Candy and Stationery Store. There were newspapers stacked up on a wooden stand next to the door. We were trying to read an article on the front page of the *Sandy Harbor Herald,* but Mr. Beebee had put a large metal paperweight over the most interesting part.

It seems that a boat belonging to one of the summer people across the bay disappeared from its mooring during the night. It was a large pleasure cruiser, but it disappeared without a trace. I was dying of curiosity.

"My father will have a copy of the paper at the store," Will said. "We can read it there. C'mon, Toria. I told Dad we'd be there before ten. He has to go out to do some errands."

"First I need a comic," Holly said.

I looked at Holly and sighed. I had promised Will I'd help out at his father's hardware store today. But Holly needed a comic book to keep her quiet.

"We'll meet you there in a few minutes," I said. Will nodded and took off down the block.

"Let's go find a comic," I said to Holly.

"Toria, can you wait for me outside? Please, please, please!" Holly begged me. "I don't want Mr. Beebee to see you with me. He hates you."

Mr. Beebee is not especially fond of me. He has been rather unfriendly ever since the day I returned a stale cherry licorice and asked for my money back. But Holly and Mr. Beebee get along quite well. She giggles at his jokes and he gives her free lollypops. It's disgusting.

"I can't let you go in there alone, Holly," I said. "Tough kids hang around Beebee's."

"Can't you pretend you don't know me?" Holly asked.

I thought about that. "Look," I finally said, "I'll pretend not to know you if you promise to pick out a comic book in a hurry. We'll go in separately. After you get your comic, you leave first, and I'll meet you down the block in front of the hardware store."

Holly thought that sounded like a good plan. She went into the candy store. I waited a few seconds and followed her inside. I went right over to the soda fountain and ordered a lemon fizz.

"Well, look who's here," I heard Mr. Beebee say to Holly. "My favorite little customer."

Holly giggled and waited for her free lollypop.

I knew it would take Holly at least ten minutes to choose a comic book. I had nothing to do so I looked around at the other people sitting at the soda fountain.

There were two men next to me drinking coffee. I knew at once that they had come off one of the pleasure boats that dock at Sandy Harbor Marina during boating season. They were sunburned. Both were wearing boating shoes and one of them had a yachting cap on his head.

"A fancy boat," I told myself. "But not a sailboat. Sailors look different. Their eyes are more windswept or something."

Both men seemed quite nervous. They kept glancing at the door. I figured they were waiting to meet someone.

"Hey, Charlie," one of them said in a gruff voice. "Do you know what this Stinkpot Harry looks like?"

Now, I am quite interested in boats. I happened to know that "stinkpot" is another word for a powerboat—but not a very nice one.

"I don't know what he looks like, but I know what he's supposed to ask for." The man with the yachting cap talked out of the corner of his mouth. He didn't talk like a fancy pleasure boater; he talked like a hoodlum!

"One lemon fizz." The girl behind the counter set my drink in front of me. "That'll be forty-five cents."

I dug into the pocket of my jeans and handed her my money. Then I sipped the lemon drink.

Holly was studying the racks of comic books as she daintily licked her green lollypop. She caught me looking at her and gave me a dirty look. I turned away.

Then I heard Holly ask Mr. Beebee, "Do you have the new Little Pieface?"

The man next to me whirled around on his

stool. The other one choked on his coffee. I looked at them. They were both staring at my sister Holly.

"What's going on?" Charlie muttered.

"The Commodore's not going to like this," the other one whispered. "Looks like Stinkpot Harry sent some kid."

"Or something's wrong," Charlie said. "If Stinkpot Harry doesn't get that message, he won't know where to find us. We better put a tail on that kid."

I almost spilled my lemon fizz. My hand was trembling. I set the glass carefully down on the counter.

"There should be a Little Pieface there," Mr. Beebee was telling Holly. "Look behind the Weirdo Comics."

A second later Holly called, "I found it!" She took it to the counter and opened her fuzzy white change purse. She paid for the comic, turned and gave me another dirty look, and walked out of the store.

The two men stood up.

"Let's go," Charlie said. He threw some change on the counter. "We can't let her out of our sight." They followed Holly out the door.

For a moment I couldn't move. I felt as if I were watching a scene in a movie. Through the window I could see my little sister Holly walking along the sidewalk, sucking a green lollypop, her head bent down over her Little Pieface . . . and she was being followed by two thugs!

I saw one of the men cross the street. He stood in front of a beauty shop and looked in the window. The other one stopped, bent down, and pretended to tie his shoelace. Then he stood up and strolled along after Holly.

"Hey, you!" Mr. Beebee called to me as I ran out the door. "Did you pay for that drink?" I nodded and ran.

I caught up with Holly and grabbed her arm.

"Quick!" I said. "We've got to run."

"Toria!" Holly pulled her arm away. "Don't you see I'm trying to read?"

I looked around. The man behind me ducked into a doorway. "Holly," I whispered, "please don't ask any questions. Just do what I say."

"You're not the boss of me," Holly said.

Then she screamed, "Toria, stop pulling!"

Will was alone behind the counter of his father's hardware store. He looked up from reading the *Sandy Harbor Herald* when I ran in the door dragging Holly.

"Toria," Will said, "what's the matter? You look scared."

"Who's scared?" I asked. "You think I'm s-s-scared just because my sister has a tail on her?"

Holly was indignant. "I do not have a tail on me. Only animals have tails. I'm telling Mommy what you just said. . . ."

"Those two men are following Holly," I told Will. "It's all because of that comic. . . ."

I repeated the conversation I had heard at the soda fountain. Will was watching the two men outside as I talked. When I finished the story, I waited for Will to laugh. I waited for him to say, "Sounds ridiculous," or, "You must be dreaming."

Will said, "I'm calling the police."

"Huh?" I followed him to the telephone at the back of the store.

"I've seen those two before," Will said. "They came in here yesterday afternoon to buy boat paint. Lots of it."

"What's wrong with buying boat paint?" I asked Will, but he was already dialing the police.

Suddenly I remembered the stolen boat. "Paint to disguise a boat?" I asked. I went back to the counter and picked up the newspaper. I read the whole article. The last paragraph read:

> Boat thieves don't just change the color of a boat. They usually redesign it and try to change the shape. Then they sell it as a brand-new boat. Sergeant Hector Small of the Sandy Harbor police said he believes that the boat thieves operate out of a secret boatyard in the area.

I was suddenly so scared I had trouble catching my breath. My mouth felt dry and I couldn't swallow. I looked at Holly. She was curled up in the store window, peacefully reading her Little Pieface.

Will hung up the phone and came back to the counter. "Sergeant Small is on his way over. We're supposed to stay right here and act natural."

"If I act too natural, I will probably faint," I muttered. I was shivering even though it was a warm day.

"Take it easy, Toria," Will said. "Besides, my father will be back any minute."

"Don't look now," I said weakly, "but I'm afraid your very next customer is Charlie the Boat Thief."

The door of the hardware store opened.

"May I help you?" Will asked Charlie.

"Uh . . . sure, kid." Charlie pushed back his yachting cap and scratched his head. He had thin yellow hair which didn't quite cover his freckled scalp. "I need some nails."

"What size?" Will asked, but Charlie wasn't paying attention. He was staring at Holly curled up in the window.

"Cute kid," he said to me. "That your little sister?" He went over to Holly, squatted down next to her and gave her a big ugly smile.

"Good comic book?" he asked her.

Holly nodded, but she didn't look up.

"Can I have a look?" Charlie asked. "I always liked Little Pieface."

"When I'm finished," Holly said coldly. "I don't like people reading over my shoulder."

The man laughed. He had a very unpleasant laugh.

"Cute kid," he said. "Look, kid, what do you say I buy that comic from you. Tell you what— I'll give you a whole dollar for it."

Holly shook her head.

Charlie wasn't smiling anymore. "C'mon," he whined. "Be a pal." His blue eyes bulged out at Holly. "Twenty dollars," he said.

Holly ignored him.

"Hey!" she suddenly said. "The Little Pieface Crossword Puzzle looks funny."

"Give that to me." Charlie reached for the comic. But, almost at once, he yelled "Ouch!" and pulled his hand back. "The kid bit me! Why, I ought to . . ."

For a moment I thought he was going to hit Holly.

"Will, please come out and help me unload the truck." Will's father was standing in the door. I was never so glad to see anyone in my life!

"Who was that?" Mr. Roberts asked as Charlie pushed past him and ran out the door.

Sergeant Small arrived a minute later. The two men had disappeared, but he was pleased to get a good description of them. He sent out the description on his car radio.

Everyone made a big fuss over Holly, even though Holly hadn't been the least bit scared. Then we stood around looking at the odd crossword puzzle in the Little Pieface.

"I'm sure it's a code," Will said.

"Never saw a code like this," Sergeant Small said.

"But you can see that someone glued a piece of paper over the real crossword puzzle," Will pointed out. "This must be the message meant for Stinkpot Harry."

"Well, it makes sense," Sergeant Small said. "Harry Byrd—otherwise known as Stinkpot

Harry—is a big-time gangster. He was operating up the coast a few years ago, but he was never caught. We think he puts up the money for the operation while these fellows do the dirty work."

"They don't know what Stinkpot Harry looks like," I said. "That's what they said at the candy store. They said he had to get the message or he wouldn't know where to find them."

"Or find where they've hidden the stolen boat," Sergeant Small said thoughtfully. "Look, I'll have to take this to the station and see if anyone can decipher it." Sergeant Small leaned over and said to Holly, "Do you mind if we borrow your comic book?"

Holly shook her head. She was enjoying all the attention. "Little Pieface was better last month," she said. Then she stuck her fingers in her mouth and gave Sergeant Small a shy smile. He patted her on the head.

"Watch out," I muttered. "It bites."

"Can we get a copy of that puzzle?" Will asked Sergeant Small.

The policeman smiled at Will. "Want to do a little detective work? Sure, come along, kids. I'll get you a copy of this. Just let us know if you come up with anything."

And I saw him wink at Mr. Roberts.

Will and I spent the whole afternoon in the library trying to figure out the meaning of the strange crossword puzzle. We went through every code and cipher book we could find. There was nothing that looked like that puzzle.

Then we went back to Will's house for dinner. After dinner we went back to work to try

The puzzle:

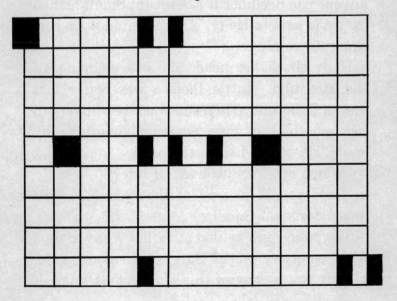

to break that code. We had the dining room to ourselves.

It got later and later. We tried everything. We tried making each square stand for a letter of the alphabet—across and down. It didn't make any sense. We tried wrapping the paper around a pencil to see if it said anything that way. We tried holding the paper in front of a mirror.

Will seemed to be bored with the puzzle. He was wandering around the dining room.

"I think I will try numbering the squares," I said. "Across and down."

"Then what?" Will asked. He looked over my shoulder. "No, I don't think it will work. This is something entirely different." Will lay down on the rug and stared up at the ceiling.

I worked for another ten minutes.

"You know, Toria," I heard Will say. "When you walk on the ceiling, it's very hard to reach that doorknob."

I ignored Will. I was too busy trying to decipher the puzzle lying in front of me on the table. "Looks like three words," I said. "The black squares are on three lines. Maybe it's dots and dashes, like the Morse code."

"Of course," Will went on, "you could balance on the ledge at the top of the door and try to reach the doorknob from there."

I turned around. "What in the world are you doing, Will?"

"Pretending to walk on the ceiling," Will said. "It's very relaxing for the mind. Come on. Try it, Toria."

I was getting nowhere with the puzzle, so I went and lay down on the dining room rug.

It is quite interesting to "walk on the ceiling." The whole room takes on another shape.

"Look," Will said. "You can sit on that beam in the corner."

"Oops," I giggled. "I almost tripped on the curtain rod."

"Watch out for the light fixture," Will said.

"All the paintings on the wall are upside down," I said.

"So is the policeman in the doorway. . . ." Will jumped to his feet. "Sorry, sir."

I gasped. "Sergeant Small!" I got up in a hurry.

"Hi, kids." Sergeant Small looked tired. "I was on my way back to the station and I thought I'd drop by to see how you were doing."

He glanced at the puzzle lying on the table. He seemed a little disappointed that we weren't working on it.

"Just taking a little break," Will said.

"We haven't had much time to work on that code ourselves," Sergeant Small said. "There's been another incident—a boat hijacking!"

"What?" Will and I stared at him.

"Yup. Johnny Engels's sailboat, the *Sea Rat,* was hijacked. He went to help two men in a rowboat. They said they had lost their oars. As soon as Johnny pulled up alongside, they climbed aboard the *Sea Rat* and grabbed him. Before he knew it, he was adrift on the rowboat and those two were aboard his *Sea Rat,* heading off into the sunset."

Sergeant Small wiped his face with a handkerchief. "Didn't pick Johnny up till after dark. But he's all right. Just furious."

"That's awful," I said. "He put so much work into that boat."

Johnny Engels is the best sailor in Sandy Harbor even though he's only eighteen. His boat, the *Sea Rat,* is the fastest boat in the bay.

"He loves that boat," Sergeant Small said. "And we're going to do our best to get it back for him. We're pretty sure one of those hijackers is your friend Charlie. The description fits perfectly."

Sergeant Small looked sadly at the puzzle lying on the table. "We sent a copy of that to our experts at regional headquarters. They can't make heads or tails out of it. They're completely stumped!"

Will and I were sitting at the table again trying to work out the code. It felt funny.

"Walking on the ceiling *is* relaxing," I said. "It's too relaxing. I can't even think anymore."

I was very sleepy. I could hardly hold my head up. "But we've got to keep working," I said.

I pushed the puzzle a little bit away from me, folded my arms on the table, and let my chin rest in my arms. My eyes kept closing.

"I guess we need a good night's sleep, Toria," Will said. "We need a fresh point of view. This is no ordinary code."

"Right." I yawned. I peeked along the table without raising my head. The puzzle was at a funny angle. The lines going across the puzzle seemed to disappear. The lines up and down seemed to stand out more. "Besides," I said sleepily, "I don't even know where it is."

"Where what is?" Will asked sharply.

"That hill," I mumbled. "I never even heard of it." My eyes would not stay open.

Will was shaking me. "Toria, you're talking in your sleep! Sit up. You're not making any sense!"

"Course I am," I murmured. "All I said was that I never heard of that particular hill."

I felt quite comfortable—cozy and safe and very sleepy. I didn't feel like sitting up.

Will sounded very far away when he said, "Toria, we know what that message says! You broke the code and you're not even awake!"

That woke me up! Can you break the code before you turn this page?

The Comic Book Caper

Will and Toria's Solution:
Will picked up the puzzle and tilted it away from him. "It's an optical illusion. When you look at it from this angle, it spells 'THIEF HILL.' You saw it before when your chin was resting on your arms."

Suddenly the words popped out at me. "Oh my goodness!" I said. "There it is! But where is Thief Hill?"

"It's the name for the cliff over Dragon's Mouth at the end of Stacey Channel," Will said. "Right beyond it is an old abandoned cove—Thief Hill Cove. No one uses it anymore. You can't even get in there at low tide. The rocks block the entrance. What a perfect place to hide a stolen boat!"

And it was. That very night police patrol boats and customs agents on Coast Guard cutters raided Thief Hill Cove. In the old fish houses standing on stilts in the water they found the two boats. They caught the boat thieves with paint all over their hands.

"Lavender paint," Johnny Engels told us the next morning. "They were trying to paint the *Sea Rat* lavender!"

Spelldown!

SANDY HARBOR, THURSDAY, JUNE 19—

"But how can anyone cheat at a spelling bee?" I asked Will.

"Toria," Will said, "those Monrose kids can find a way to cheat at anything."

Will and I were walking home from school. Today was the last day of school. I felt like throwing my books in the air and shouting for joy, but I didn't. I knew Will was right to be worried.

Tomorrow is the Countywide Spelling Bee Championship. It will be held at the Sandy Harbor Theater. The best speller from every school in our county will be there. The bee is sponsored every year by our local newspaper, the *Sandy Harbor Herald*.

We are very excited about it. Our friend Chuck is the champion speller from our school. He is also a trusted member of the T*A*C*K team.

"Look, Will," I said. "Lester is the only kid at Monrose with any brains at all, and he will be up on the stage. He is the only kid at Monrose who can spell 'cat.' The rest of them are too busy being bullies—like dear old Red Jamieson. They're not smart enough to cheat at a spelling bee."

"What if Red is sitting in the audience with a dictionary?" Will said. "And what if he coaches Lester . . ."

"No one can see into the audience," I said. "Remember? The stage is flooded with bright lights. It is impossible to see out. Besides that, the panel of judges sits in front to make sure there is no funny business."

"But don't you see?" Will said. "Bright lights, dark auditorium . . . those are the very conditions magicians and mind readers work under. There are dozens of ways to communicate with someone like Red sitting there with a dictionary. They could use signals—lights, sounds, little pulses that go through wires to the stage— even smells! It's done all the time."

"Will, I think you're overdoing this a little," I said. "And you're forgetting one important thing."

"What's that?" Will asked me.

"Red probably doesn't even know how to look up words in a dictionary," I said.

FRIDAY, JUNE 20 —

9:45 A.M.

There is an air of excitement in the lobby of the Sandy Harbor Theater. Everyone is standing around wishing their contestants good luck. The contestants are wearing numbers around their necks. Chuck is number eleven.

Will came in wearing a new shirt. I could tell it was new because the sleeves reached all the way down to his wrists and it looked a bit stiff and creased. It was exactly the same green-and-blue plaid as all Will's other shirts.

"How do you like it?" he asked me.

"Nice plaid," I said.

Just then the Monrose bus pulled up. We could hear them singing:

> We are the Monrose Monsters,
> known both far and wide.
> We are the Monrose Monsters,
> fighting for our side . . .

"They sing at a spelling bee?" a girl from another school asked me.

"Let's hope that's all they do," I said.

"How do you feel?" Will asked Chuck.

"Fine," Chuck said. "I'm not even nervous."

The Monsters were pretty well behaved. They stood in a corner of the lobby and gave their top speller Lester hard little punches in the arm.

"Hi, Will! Hi, Toria!" Chuck's mother appeared. She looked very proud. Her hair had been done at the beauty parlor.

"Chuck, dear," she said. "I just want you to know that, whatever happens, we will always be proud of you."

She went on like that for a while. Chuck began to look nervous.

"Now," she finally said, "I'm going to find a seat nice and close. If you get nervous, just remember: *Your mother is right there!*"

Chuck swallowed hard. "Thanks, Mom," he mumbled.

She went inside. Chuck said, "You don't suppose my mother is working for Monrose?"

We laughed. That made Chuck feel better.

Suddenly Rachel came running up. Rachel is in our class. Her eyes were round and she was out of breath.

"Guess what Red Jamieson told me to tell you?" Rachel said to Chuck.

"Why don't we take a nice little walk, Rachel," I suggested. "You know, look at movie posters, count seats . . ." I didn't think Rachel was *good* for Chuck.

But Rachel was already going through a long list of things Red was planning to do to Chuck if Chuck won. It was an unattractive and gory list, so I won't go into it.

"If I were you," Rachel told Chuck, "I would try to lose this spelling bee. If you're smart you'll miss a word in the first round."

Chuck was pale. He turned to Will. "My mind just went blank. I won't be able to spell anything. I just lost my appetite for words."

"Don't worry," Rachel said. "I told that Red Jamieson. I really let him have it."

"What did you say?" Will asked her.

"I said, 'You wouldn't dare!'" Rachel seemed very pleased with herself.

"Rachel," Will said, "I hate to be critical, but that is the worst possible thing you could have said to Red. Red loves dares. He loves to make bets."

"I'm not finished." Rachel seemed a little hurt. "Listen to what I said next. It's much better. I said, 'You wouldn't dare. Chuck's mother is here.'"

"Oh, no," Chuck groaned.

"Take it easy, Chuck," Will said. He turned to Rachel. "What did Red say to that?"

"Not much," Rachel thought for a second. "He asked me which one was Chuck's mother and I showed him, and let's see . . . Red said something else, but I can't remember what."

"Think, Rachel," I said gently. "What did Red say next?"

"Oh, I remember," Rachel said. "He said it isn't often he gets a crack at someone's mother, too." Rachel skipped off to find herself a seat in the theater.

"So that's the plan." Will seemed disappointed. "Nothing clever. Nothing subtle. Just plain old threats of physical violence."

"But do you know something about threats like that?" Chuck asked Will.

"What?" Will asked.

"They really work." Chuck was sweating.

"Chuck," Will said, "your job is to win this spelling bee. Toria and I will make sure that

Red doesn't bother you when it's over. He'll be so busy he won't even notice you leave."

"Promise?" Chuck asked.

"I'll do better than that. I'll guarantee it. Now spell 'guarantee.' "

"G-U-A-R-A-N-T-E-E." Chuck seemed more relaxed.

10:10 A.M.

The spelling bee has begun. Harrison Parks, the editor of the *Sandy Harbor Herald,* gave a speech about how our young people are our nation's most valuable resources, and then the first contestant stepped up to the microphone. She was so short, she had trouble reaching it.

Mr. Parks gave her the first word, "friend."

No one missed a word in the first round. The words seemed pretty easy to me, but Will whispered, "Those kids are good. I already missed five." (Will is not the best speller in our class.)

When Chuck spelled the word "receive" correctly, his mother, who was sitting next to me, burst into wild applause.

"No applause until the end of the round, please," Harrison Parks announced.

The words in the second round were harder.

"Have you thought of anything yet?" I whispered to Will.

Will shook his head. "I know one thing, though," he said. "It's got to be a bet. Red loves to bet. But I need to think of a bet that fits his mood."

I turned and looked at Red, who was standing in the back of the auditorium.

"His mood is mean, Will," I said. "Real mean."

It was Chuck's turn to spell. "Handkerchief," Mr. Parks said.

"H-A-N-D- ..." Chuck spells very slowly. That is his style. Every speller seems to have their own style.

"Handkerchief!" Will suddenly said. "That's it! Toria, can you get me one?"

I leaned over and asked Chuck's mother if I could borrow her handkerchief.

"Of course, dear," she said. "This is awfully moving, isn't it?" She thought I was crying.

I handed it to Will. He nodded, and without looking at me, tucked it into his pocket.

11:15 A.M.

We are up to the "spelldown." There are only two contestants left — Lester and Chuck.

"Miscellany," Mr. Parks's voice boomed.

Lester left out the "c." Chuck spelled it correctly. I was about to cheer when Mr. Parks said Chuck had to spell another word correctly, too. If Chuck missed, he said, it would be a tie. "Separate," he said.

"S-E-P- . . ." Chuck paused. There wasn't a sound in the theater.

"That's easy," Will whispered. "Even I can spell that."

"A . . ." Chuck went on.

"Oh, no!" Will said. "He missed. It's an 'e'!"

But Chuck was right. He spelled the rest of the word. Chuck was the winner!

The photographer from the *Herald* dashed onto the stage to take Chuck's picture.

"I suppose he's going to want to take my picture, too," Chuck's mother sighed.

"Let's go, Toria." Will was dragging me out of the auditorium.

We found Red and two of his friends in the lobby of the theater.

"Wait till I get ahold of that creep," Red was saying. "I'll show him how to spell *pain!*"

"You sure will, Red," one of his buddies said proudly. "You'll spell him right in the nose."

"Oh, Red," Will said. "Could I speak to you a minute?"

Red looked down at Will. "What d'ya want, creep?"

"Look, Red, forget Chuck. How would you like a chance to punch me?" Will said.

"Huh?" Red asked.

"And I won't even fight back," Will told him. "But on one condition. If you miss me, you don't get a second chance."

"I never miss," Red said. "Are you crazy?"

"Red never misses," Red's buddies told Will. "Are you crazy, kid?"

"Now, wait a minute," Red said. "Are you telling me that you're going to let me take a swing at you—and you're not even going to fight back? What's the catch?"

"That's easy," one of his friends said. "He's going to run as fast as he can."

"No, I'm not," Will said. "I will stand perfectly still."

Red was getting interested. "How far away will you be?" he asked. "On the other side of town?" And he laughed.

"Nope," Will said. "I'll be very close . . . within punching distance."

Chuck and his mother came into the lobby. Chuck's mother was telling a reporter what a good speller she had been when she was a kid. Chuck took one look at us and tried to get his mother to hurry. When they went out through the big glass door, I breathed a sigh of relief. Red hadn't even noticed them.

"How close will you be standing?" Red had grabbed Will by the front of his shirt. "This close?" he growled.

"Just about," Will said. Red let him go.

"I'll show you how close we'll be." Will pulled Chuck's mother's handkerchief out of his pocket. "We'll both be standing on this handkerchief."

"That's pretty close," Red admitted.

"But I get to lay it down," Will said.

"Go right ahead," Red said. "This is fun." He was already winding up for the punch.

"Just one chance," Will reminded him.

I looked around the lobby. There was no one around except Will, the Monrose Monsters, and me!

"Will," I whispered, "are you *sure* you know what you are doing?"

Will nodded. "He'll never touch me."

Will knew exactly what he was doing. We got out of that theater in one piece. Can you guess what Will did?

Spelldown!

Will's Solution:

"How did you do it?" Chuck asked Will afterward. "How did you avoid getting punched by Red?"

"First tell me how you knew how to spell 'separate,'" Will said. "I was sure it had an 'e' in it."

"'Separate' has 'a rat' in it," Chuck said. "You can always remember that way."

"Terrific!" Will said. "A rat!"

"Well?" Chuck said. "Go ahead. Tell me."

But Will was still thinking over the "rat" in "separate." I had to tell Chuck the story.

". . . and you should have seen Red's face." I was laughing. "Red was winding up for the big punch, and Will carefully laid the handkerchief down under the glass door of the lobby. Half of the handkerchief was on the inside and half was on the outside of the door. Will stood on the edge of the handkerchief outside the theater. Red was inside. We waved to Red through the glass door . . . and ran!"

"Red waved back," Will said. "Remember?"

"That wasn't a wave," I said to Will. "No one waves with their fist!"

The Great Blueberry Pie Robbery

MY HOUSE, FRIDAY, JULY 4—

Will and his younger brother Cyrus are coming to our house this afternoon. They are invited to stay for a cookout tonight.

It's been raining hard all day. Will and Cyrus arrived after lunch. They were soaking wet.

"Sorry we can't have that cookout," my mother said. "But I just love this weather. It's the perfect day to curl up with a nice cozy mystery story."

Will pulled a book out from under his yellow raincoat. "Funny you should say that, Mrs. Gardner," Will said. "I brought along a mystery I've been reading."

"And I brought you a present, Mrs. Gardner," Will's little brother Cyrus said.

At the word "present," my little sister Holly appeared from nowhere and stood there staring down at the shopping bag Cyrus was carrying.

My mother's face lit up when she saw the

book Will was reading, "Oh. Will, you're reading *The Murder of Roger Ackroyd!* Isn't it terrific? Have you guessed who did it yet?"

"No," Will said. "But I have an idea."

"MOTHER!" Holly said. "Didn't you hear? Cyrus brought you a present."

My mother looked in the shopping bag. "How nice," she said. "Two quarts of fresh blueberries. . . . You know, Will, speaking of mysteries, I'm reading a great one. . . ."

"My mother loves the blueberries," Holly told Cyrus. "She loves them so much she is going to make a blueberry pie out of them."

"Oh, boy." Cyrus poked Will. "Did you hear that? Mrs. Gardner's making a pie!"

"I am?" My mother smiled at Cyrus. "That's not a bad idea."

2:30 P.M.

My mother is curled up in her easy chair in the den reading *The Greene Murder Case.* Will is lying on the floor reading his mystery, and I am trying to read a mystery story, too. I don't even know the name of it. I keep reading the same sentence over and over. . . .

"I believe," the great detective said, "that everyone in this room has something to hide."

I just can't concentrate. All I can think about is my mom's blueberry pie baking in the oven. The smell is driving me crazy.

4:15 P.M.

Time is going so slowly. My mother just went to put the pie into the refrigerator.

"One of my best," she said and went back to reading her mystery story.

My little sister Holly has been in the living room all afternoon playing the piano. She can only play one piece—"Chopsticks." I haven't seen Cyrus for a while. He must be out in my father's workshed. My father, known to us as Popsy, is a famous amateur magician. He loves to have an audience for his magic tricks.

I stared out at the rain and listened to the sound of my mother and Will turning pages.

All I can think about is blueberry pie. I don't know how I'll ever last until dinner.

"I think I'll read upstairs," I said. "It's hard to concentrate when Holly is playing the piano."

No one answered so I left the room.

As I passed through the kitchen, I peeked into the refrigerator. The blueberry pie was on the bottom shelf.

It was an open pie with strips of crust woven across the top. It was the most beautiful—the most luscious—pie I have ever seen.

Then I noticed there was a little too much filling in one spot. "It doesn't look right oozing out like that," I told myself.

I picked up a long-handled spoon that was lying on the counter. Carefully I scooped out a little filling. It was delicious!

I closed the refrigerator door gently and left the kitchen.

Holly saw me when I got to the landing at the foot of the stairs.

"Toria!" she yelled. "Listen to this."

I waited patiently while she played "Chopsticks" all the way through. Then I fled up the stairs and into my room. I closed the door and turned on the radio to drown out the sound of the piano.

4:30 P.M.

My watch must have stopped. It feels as if it's been 4:30 for hours and hours. I decided to go down to the kitchen and check with the kitchen clock.

I didn't want to get mixed up with Holly

again, so I took a special route. I climbed over the bannister and let myself down onto a table in the hall. Then I tiptoed down the hallway and into the kitchen.

The kitchen clock said 4:30, too. Slowly I turned around. I stared at the refrigerator door. I don't remember anything else. . . .

4:45 P.M.

I'm back in my room now. I keep hearing this crackling sound. It seems to be coming from Holly's room. But Holly is still downstairs. I peeked into her room. It was empty.

I bent down and picked up a broken potato chip. Holly is not allowed to keep potato chips in her room. I put the pieces in my shirt pocket for future reference.

5:50 P.M.

Only ten minutes until dinner. Hooray!

6:45 P.M.

Dinner was delicious. We had a wonderful chicken salad my mom made this morning. Everyone ate a lot except Cyrus.

Cyrus kept pushing food around on his plate. "Saving up for the pie?" Popsy asked him.

"I guess I'm not too hungry," Cyrus whispered. "I don't think I can eat any pie."

All of a sudden there was a clatter in the kitchen and a terrible scream.

"My pie!" my mother shrieked.

We looked at one another. Then we ran into the kitchen.

The pie was on the kitchen counter. It looked very strange.

"The filling's been dug out!" my mother said in horror. "There are holes all over my pie!"

When I looked through the strips of crust, there was no filling at all in some places. I could see right down to the bottom crust. In one place I could see the pie plate.

My mother put her hands on her hips. "All right," she said. "Who did it? Who ruined my

pie? Speak up. I want to know right this minute."

She glared at each one of us. "So, no one's talking, eh?"

My father gently covered the remains of the pie with a cake tin. It was very sad to watch.

"I think," my mother said, "this calls for an investigation!"

7:15 P.M.

We were all seated around the dining room table staring down at our empty dessert plates.

"I believe," my mother began, "that the crime was committed by someone sitting right at this table."

Everyone gasped. I wasn't a bit surprised, but, since everyone else was gasping, I gasped, too.

Will stood up. "Mrs. Gardner," he said, "the first thing we have to do is to find out where each person was between the hours of four and six o'clock. Each person has to establish an alibi. You and I were in the den, of course, reading mystery stories the whole time. If anyone else can prove they were someplace else during that time, they will have an alibi, too."

"I was in the living room playing 'Chopsticks,'" Holly said quickly.

"She never stopped." My mother groaned.

I was next. "I was up in my room," I said, "playing my radio."

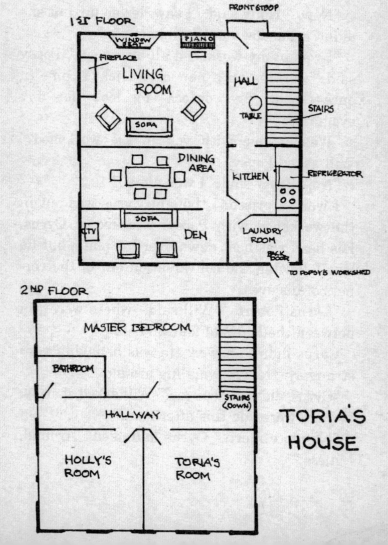

1ST FLOOR

FRONT STOOP

WINDOW SEAT

PIANO

FIREPLACE

LIVING ROOM

HALL

STAIRS

TABLE

SOFA

DINING AREA

KITCHEN

REFRIGERATOR

SOFA

TV

DEN

LAUNDRY ROOM

BACK DOOR

TO POPSY'S WORKSHED

2ND FLOOR

MASTER BEDROOM

BATHROOM

STAIRS (DOWN)

HALLWAY

HOLLY'S ROOM

TORIA'S ROOM

TORIA'S HOUSE

"Do you have any witnesses?" Will asked me.

"Er . . . I guess not," I said sadly.

"But I would have seen her if she came down the stairs," Holly said.

"And did you?" my mother asked her.

"Nope," Holly said. "I saw her go up, but she didn't come down until dinnertime."

"I was in my workshed all afternoon," Popsy said, "working on a new card trick. I came in once—about five o'clock—to look for my eyeglasses."

"Was anyone with you in the workshed?" Will asked Popsy.

"No," Popsy said. "I was alone."

I was surprised. I thought Cyrus was out in the workshed with Popsy. I looked at Cyrus. His head was bent down over his plate, but he was following the conversation out of the corners of his eyes.

"Cyrus Roberts," Will said, "where were you between the hours of four and six?"

Cyrus didn't answer. He was behaving very strangely. He was wiggling around.

"Cyrus, did you hear me?" Will asked sharply. "Where were you this afternoon?"

"No place much," Cyrus mumbled. "Around, I guess."

Holly shouted with glee, "He did it! Cyrus dug up the pie! Don't you see? That's why he wasn't hungry. He was stuffed up with blueberry filling. Cyrus is guilty!"

Cyrus certainly looked guilty. But there was something wrong. He looked too guilty. Suddenly I thought I knew what had happened.

"Will," I said, "do you mind if I take over this investigation—just for a moment?"

"Go right ahead, Toria." Will looked surprised.

I paced over to the window and stood there looking out into the darkness. Then I said in a quiet voice: "I believe Cyrus is innocent."

"But he doesn't have an alibi!" Holly shouted.

I whirled around and faced the table. "No one has an airtight alibi," I said. "There is something wrong with everyone's story. I believe everyone in this room has something to hide."

"Wow! Isn't she terrific?" my mother whispered. "Better than the detective in my book."

I pretended not to hear that remark.

"Now, my own alibi depends on the fact that Holly was sitting at the piano the whole time. If I had left my room, she would have seen me on the landing at the foot of the stairs. But what if . . ."

I stopped. I knew I had to be careful. I didn't want to prove Cyrus innocent by getting myself into trouble. And I was sure I had tasted only one or two little blueberries.

"What if *what?*" Will asked.

"What if Holly didn't see me come down the stairs. What if she didn't see me because . . . *she wasn't there?*"

"I get it." Will was excited. "She was playing a tape of 'Chopsticks' and sneaking into the kitchen."

Will was too quick for me.

"No, no, no," I said. "Our tape recorder's broken anyway. Don't you see? Holly's alibi, in turn, depends on two *ear*-witnesses—Mom and Will—sitting in the den, listening to Holly play. But what if, for any reason, they were unable to hear . . ."

"What are you getting at, Toria?" my mother asked me nervously.

"Mom, is it not true . . ." I began slowly, "that you have been known to *put cotton in your ears when Holly is playing the piano?*"

Mom and Will glanced quickly at each other. Then they both looked down. Their faces turned bright red.

"Aha!" I said. "I was right. You both had cotton in your ears."

Holly's eyes filled with tears. "You weren't even listening. You said I played beautifully and you weren't even listening."

"The little I heard, Holly," my mother murmured, "was really quite lovely."

"I'm trying to show that everyone is still a suspect," I explained, "even Mom and Will. Now, everyone knows the way those two read mysteries. Do you think either of them would have noticed if the other one left the room?"

"They wouldn't notice if the house fell down," my father said. He looked at me curiously.

"What about my alibi, Toria?" he asked.

"Not bad, Popsy, except for one thing. You said you were working on card tricks all afternoon, right? You only came into the house once to look for your eyeglasses. . . ."

Popsy nodded.

"But, Popsy," I said, *"you need your eyeglasses to do card tricks!"*

"Good point." Popsy laughed.

"Toria," Will said, "you still haven't proven that Cyrus is innocent."

I reached into my pocket and placed the broken potato chip on the dining room table.

"My Tater Ruffles!" Holly shrieked. "What are you doing with my Tater Ruffles? I didn't even open them yet."

"Holly, what were *you* doing with Tater Ruffles?" my mother asked coldly.

"These were on the floor of Holly's room," I went on. "At the time I did not think of looking under the bed, but, if I had, I believe I would have discovered Cyrus—quietly eating Tater Ruffles."

Cyrus broke down. "I couldn't stop," he confessed. "I just couldn't stop eating them."

"You see," I said, "that explains where Cyrus was. It also explains why he wasn't hungry."

"I had a whole Twin Packie under my bed," Holly wailed, "and he ate them all up. Mom!"

"You'll get no sympathy from me, Holly," Mom said. "You know you are forbidden to have food of any kind in your room."

Holly clamped her mouth shut and glared at Cyrus.

"Toria, you're amazing!" Will was looking at me with admiration. "But where do you suggest we go from here?"

"Let me see." I felt pretty clever. "I know. What about evidence? You know, fingerprints or something like that."

"Terrific!" Will said. "Of course, the pie thief must have used a weapon—a spoon or a fork to get into that pie. Fingerprints!"

"Mouth prints, too," Cyrus suggested.

I was sorry I had opened my mouth.

Mom gasped. "Oh, no! There was a spoon lying right on the counter, but I washed it. I dried it, too."

"Too bad," I said a little too quickly. "That takes care of that. Forget I said it. Now, isn't it possible we are overlooking the possibility that this was the work of an outsider—an outside raccoon or something?"

Will shook his head. "No, Toria. I like your idea of finding physical evidence. Wait a minute! What if the evidence is right here? Right under our noses?"

"Don't you think we should . . . um . . ."—my voice got fainter—"explore this raccoon theory?"

"No," Will said. "I know how we can get foolproof evidence . . ."

All at once I knew, too. I felt trapped. Can you guess how to find the pie thief before you turn this page?

The Great Blueberry Pie Robbery

Will's Solution:

"But I only had a little," I protested. "Just to even it off."

"I must have tasted that filling more than I realized," my mother admitted. "But I had to test it."

"I don't even remember doing it," Popsy confessed.

Holly was furious. "Just because my teeth and tongue are blue doesn't prove a thing," she insisted.

"You see," Will said, "the blueberry stain will remain on the teeth and tongue for hours. It is direct physical evidence. It is proof!"

"Wait a minute, Will," I said. "Don't you think you should smile and show us your tongue, too?"

"Is that really necessary?" Will asked.

We all nodded.

"Wow!" Cyrus said, staring at Will's blue tongue. "Everyone's guilty but me. I only had salt on my tongue."

There was a growl from Holly.

Cyrus was very proud until he realized he was the only one who didn't get any pie.

"How about some nice pieces of crust with vanilla ice cream?" my mother asked us.

T*A*C*K into Danger

This has been the most exciting summer of my whole life. On top of everything else, my best friend Abby arrived today. She is spending the rest of the summer at her grandmother's house—right here in Sandy Harbor.

Will and I were sitting on my front stoop when Abby showed up. She was wearing a bright pink terrycloth sunsuit, and her hair was in a neat ponytail tied with a pink ribbon.

"Abby!" I hugged her.

"It's great you're going to be staying for the whole summer," Will said to her.

Abby brushed some dirt off her white socks and sat down on the stoop. "Well," she said slowly, "I *am* glad to see you two, of course, but . . ."

"But what?" I asked her.

"It's just that I'm missing so many things in Pleasantville. You see, every day the kids go to this fabulous swimming pool, and ... well, anyway, next week is the big pool party. And I'm going to miss it!"

Abby looked miserable. "Besides," she said, "you know how it is in Sandy Harbor in the summer. Nothing ever happens. There's nothing to do!"

Will and I looked at each other. Will stretched out his legs and leaned back on the stoop.

"I guess you've got a point," he said to Abby. "It's been pretty quiet around here—except, of course, for that gang of boat thieves who were prowling around. . . ."

I yawned. "Yeah—a few hijackings, secret codes in comic books—that sort of thing."

Abby's mouth fell open. "Boat thieves? Secret codes? What are you talking about?"

We told her about The Comic Book Caper. "Are you making this up?" she kept asking. But when we finished, she said, "I don't believe it—and I had to miss the whole thing. I miss everything!" She thought for a moment. "Well, what are you working on now? Does T*A*C*K have a new case?"

"No time for crime," Will said.

"Nope." I sighed. "It's so difficult to find time

for anything when you're taking sailing lessons every single day."

"Sailing lessons?" Abby stared at us.

"It was our reward for helping to catch those boat thieves," I said. "Johnny Engels is a great teacher. He lets us sail the *Sea Rat* ourselves. He just sits there. If we look like we're going to get into trouble, he just talks to us in this quiet voice. He never gets excited. He hardly ever touches the tiller."

"What's that?" Abby asked me. "What's a tiller?"

"That stick at the back of the sailboat. You steer with it," I told her.

"You know, Toria," Will said, "Johnny was saying just yesterday that we really need another crew member to help us sail."

"I know," I said. "Someone to handle the jib."

Abby stood up.

"Where are you going?" Will asked her.

"I'm going to ask Grandma Abigail if I can learn to handle the jib—whatever *that* is." Abby started to run. Will and I ran to catch up with her.

"You might not like sailing," Will said. "All you do at first is to learn to tie knots . . ."

"Spend a lot of time scraping barnacles off

the bottom of the boat." I was running alongside of Abby laughing. "Then you have to learn all the names for things. You have to learn a whole new language—sailing language."

Abby stopped in front of her grandmother's house. She grabbed my arm. "Teach me some words right now," she demanded. "Teach me to say something in sailing language."

"Let me see," I said. "The right side of the boat is called starboard and the left side is port . . . when you're facing forward."

"Starboard and port," Abby said. "I've got it." And she climbed the steps to her grandmother's house two at a time.

DOVER INLET, SATURDAY, AUGUST 16 —

1300 HOURS
(They use a 24-hour clock on the sea;
1300 hours is the same as 1 P.M.)

I was at the tiller sailing the boat up Dover Inlet. It was a beautiful clear day. There was a light breeze. The wind was coming over our port side. I pulled in the mainsail a little and headed the boat more into the wind.

"Ready about?" I called.

"Yes, Toria, sir," Will called back.

I pushed the tiller all the way over to the other side. "Hard to leeward!"

The boat turned into the wind. The mainsail flapped and then swung over to the other side and filled out.

"Pull in the jib a little, Abby," I said.

Quickly Abby pulled in the small sail in front of the mainsail. Abby is learning fast. "Okay?" she asked me.

Now the wind was coming over the starboard side. We were on a "starboard tack." *T*A*C*K learns to tack,* I thought.

I looked at Johnny. He sat comfortably in the sailboat. He didn't say anything—just gave me a slight nod. I knew I had done a good job of "coming about."

STACEY CHANNEL, 1405 HOURS (2:05 P.M.)

Will is sailing the boat now. We are sailing with the wind almost directly behind us. Our sails are all the way out.

"Want to try a jibe?" Johnny asked Will.

Will shook his head. "Don't feel I'm ready yet."

"Toria?" Johnny asked.

I shook my head. I was afraid.

Jibing about is the opposite of coming about: You turn the boat when the wind is behind you. It can be very tricky. If you jibe by mistake, it can be quite dangerous. The wind will suddenly catch the other side of the sail, and the sail comes over so fast it can tip the whole boat over. It is also dangerous because the boom—the heavy pole along the bottom of the sail—can hit you in the head and knock you out. You have to be sure to duck in time.

But learning to jibe is necessary if you want to learn to sail. You just want to be able to control the jibe. And you want to do it on purpose!

"Prepare to jibe . . . jibe ho!" Johnny jibed the boat around smoothly. We all breathed a sigh of relief. He gave the tiller back to Will.

"Now what?" he asked us. "What do you want to do today?"

"Johnny," Will said, "could we go someplace new? Someplace we haven't been before?"

"Where do you want to go?" Johnny asked.

Will pointed toward the shore. "We could explore Spider Creek," he said.

"Don't know it very well," Johnny said. "It's not on my chart, and from what I remember it's not very well marked."

"Oh, please can we take Spider Creek?" we begged. It sounded like such an adventure.

Johnny looked at his watch. It was only 1430 hours (2:30 P.M.). He looked up at the sky. It was a beautiful sunny day. Then he turned and looked at the grassy marshlands and the entrance to Spider Creek.

"Well," he said, "there should be enough water in there. And I guess you'll get some practice tacking. Spider Creek twists and turns all over the place."

SPIDER CREEK, 1530 HOURS (3:30 P.M.)

Spider Creek is not all that interesting. No houses or anything. Just tall grass on either side. Everything looks the same.

"I thought we passed that place an hour ago," Abby whispered to me. She was shivering. The sun had gone behind some clouds.

I handed Abby my sweatshirt.

SPIDER CREEK, 1600 HOURS (4 P.M.)

"Should I turn back?" Will asked Johnny. Will was sailing the boat. "That fog sure came up fast."

Fog had closed in on us.

Johnny seemed worried. "Are you all right?" he asked us.

I tried not to let him see that my teeth were chattering. "Just fine," I said.

"This is fun," Abby said in a shaky voice.

"No, it's not," Johnny said sharply. "It's dangerous. Listen. Up ahead, somewhere, there's a Coast Guard station. I'm not sure exactly where it is, but I think we'd better find it and pull in there. We can call your parents to tell them you're all right."

We sailed in silence. It was eerie in the fog. We wouldn't see the shore until we were almost on top of it. All of a sudden this giant grass would appear out of nowhere. Then Will would shout, "Ready about!" and turn the boat, "Hard to leeward!"

We had to do a lot of tacking back and forth. The wind was unsteady and shifty. Then it died down completely. We waited.

When a slight breeze started up again, it was coming from behind. Will let out the sail almost all the way. Abby let out the jib. We were running before the wind. "Please don't jibe, Will," I whispered to myself.

Suddenly I wanted to go home very badly.

Just then, we heard the sound of a motor. But, in a fog, it is impossible to tell which way sounds are coming from.

"Maybe we could ask them to take us to the Coast Guard station," Abby suggested.

"Good idea," Johnny said. "But where is that motorboat? It might be heading away from us."

We peered into the fog. The sound of the motorboat got louder.

"I see it!" I shouted.

"I don't see a boat," Will said.

"Not the boat!" I said. "The sign. There's a sign up ahead. Spider Creek comes to an end and splits into two channels. There's a sign with three arrows on it!"

Johnny saw it, too. "We'll have to get much closer to read it," he said. "But we can't be too far from that Coast Guard station now."

"Which way is it?" Abby asked.

"I don't remember," Johnny said, "but the sign will tell us."

We could still hear the motorboat. "They're going awfully fast," Johnny said. "We're better off sailing to the station ourselves than taking a tow from a boat that goes that fast in a fog!"

Then I saw it. The bow of a large motorboat

loomed out of the fog. And it was headed right for our port side!

"Will," I said, "there's-a-boat-gonna-smash-into-us." I pointed.

Will saw it coming, too. "Help me, Toria," he said. "Pull in the mainsail as fast as you can. Prepare to jibe!"

I did what I was told. "Jibe ho!" Will called, and he turned the boat out of the way of the motorboat. There was a jerk on the sail. Then, as smoothly as possible, I let the sail swing out to the other side.

"That motorboat just missed us!" Abby said.

"Beautiful jibe," Johnny said. "Couldn't have done better myself." Then he turned to stare at the motorboat.

"Slow down!" he yelled to the people in the motorboat. He motioned with his arm up and down.

"They're waving at us," Abby said in a dull voice. "They think we're being friendly."

"Watch out for their wake," Johnny said. The motorboat was making big waves.

There was a loud crack up ahead.

"I don't believe it," Johnny said. "They hit the sign. Knocked it right over. Broke it!" He stared in disbelief.

When the first wave from the motorboat hit our boat, everything seemed to happen at once :

Our boat began to rock violently from side to side . . .

Abby, Will, and I ducked when we saw the boom come swinging over . . .

and Johnny turned just in time to get smacked in the nose with the boom.

Will quickly turned the boat all the way around and into the wind. The sails flapped and we came to a stop. We looked in horror at Johnny.

Johnny had his hand over his nose. Blood was oozing out between his fingers.

"Afraid my nose is broken," Johnny mumbled.

"We'll get you to the Coast Guard station right away," Will promised.

"You can't," Johnny moaned. "They knocked the sign down."

"But it's floating in the water," Abby said. "We'll just put it back."

"But we'll never be able to tell which way the arrows are supposed to point!" Johnny's voice was cracking. He was a mess. He was holding his T-shirt up over his nose, trying to stop the blood.

"Everything is under control," Will said. "I am going to sail around that sign and come up into the wind. Toria and Abby will haul it up out of the water. It might be heavy."

"But we'll never be able to figure it out!" Johnny was choking back tears of pain.

"Please stop talking, Johnny," I said firmly. "Talking is not good for a broken nose."

Johnny was quiet for a moment. Then he mumbled, "Blood all over my paint job."

"That's right." Abby patted his shoulder. "Now, you worry about your paint job and we'll take care of the sign." She gave Will and me a desperate look.

Somehow or other we managed to pull that broken sign out of the water. We turned it around and around. To me the situation looked hopeless. Here is what it looked like:

We didn't want to worry Johnny, so we had to be very careful what we said.

"That's great!" I said. "We're only half a mile from the Coast Guard station."

(But I was thinking, *So near and yet so far. We'll be sailing in circles while Johnny bleeds.*)

"If worse comes to worst," Will said, "we can always find the post and see how the splinters fit together." (But I knew Will was thinking, *That sign broke below water level! We'll never be able to find the rest of the post.*)

"And, of course," Abby said, "we could go half a mile each way and see where the Coast Guard station turns up." (But we were all thinking, *Takes too much time. We might never even see it in this fog. We might go right past it. We have to take the right turn now. This is an emergency!*)

Will twisted the sign slowly around.

"I know the right way," he suddenly said.

He took the tiller again. "Watch your jib, Abby," he called, and he headed the boat up the channel to the right. "This is the way to the Coast Guard station."

"Of course it is," Abby and I agreed. *(And boy, did we ever hope Will was right!)*

Will was right. Before we knew it, we were at the Coast Guard station. How did Will know which way to twist that sign?

T*A*C*K into Danger

Will's Solution:

When we got to the Coast Guard station, Johnny got medical treatment right away. His nose wasn't broken—just badly bruised.

"Since I'm giving you sailing lessons," Johnny said, "you can give me a few thinking lessons. How did you ever figure out which way that sign was supposed to go?"

"All I did was turn the sign, so that the arrow that said Spider Creek pointed back the way we came from," Will told him. "That way the other arrows had to be right."

Zoo T*A*C*K-tics

Abby and I were in my kitchen making peanut-butter-and-banana sandwiches.

"It's the big thing in Pleasantville," Abby told me. "Wait until you taste them."

The doorbell rang, and a few seconds later, Will walked into the kitchen.

"Guess who's here?" Will said. "Guess who's visiting us?"

"Who?" Abby asked.

"My cousin Nicholas . . ." Will said.

I had never heard Will talk about his cousin Nicholas before.

". . . and you should see the way Nicholas's mother—my Aunt Betsy—treats him. It's terrible. I can't stand it. She babies him all the time. She has no respect for his mind."

"How old is your cousin Nicholas?" I asked.

"Two and a half," Will said, "but he's very

advanced for his age. I told my Aunt Betsy he needed more intellectual challenges, so we're talking him to the Lakewood Park Zoo today. Do you want to come?"

"Abby, too?" I asked.

"Of course," Will said. "Chuck's coming. His family got back from vacation last night."

Will sat down at the kitchen table and watched us make sandwiches. "You see," he went on, "Nicholas has never been to a zoo. We would be in charge of introducing him to the world of animals. We would be his tour guides."

"Sounds like fun," I said.

Will stood up. "Great!" he said. "We'll pick you up in an hour."

"We'll bring the picnic," Abby said. "We'll make plenty of peanut-butter-and-banana sandwiches."

"Is that what that is?" Will asked.

"Abby," I said, "just to be safe—why don't we make a few peanut-butter-and-grapefruit-marmalade sandwiches."

"How about one or two peanut-butter-and-nothing sandwiches?" Will suggested.

Will's Aunt Betsy drove us to the zoo in her station wagon. Her little boy Nicholas is full of energy. He has bright red hair and green eyes. He was dressed in a light blue sailor blouse and white shorts. Before we climbed into the back of the station wagon, Will made us promise not to use any baby talk when speaking to Nicholas.

"He's perfectly capable of intelligent conversation," Will said. "You see, if you treat him as an equal, he will behave as an equal."

Chuck, Abby, and I took turns holding Nicholas on our laps while he pulled our noses and laughed. Then Nicholas got into our picnic basket and took one bite of every sandwich. The rest of each sandwich he squeezed in his fist and watched banana and peanut butter squish out through his fingers.

When we arrived at the zoo, Nicholas was busy fingerpainting with peanut butter on the station wagon window.

"Isn't it amazing?" Will asked us. "Just look at how many things he thinks of doing with a simple peanut butter sandwich."

"He's very creative," Chuck said.

Aunt Betsy was not impressed with Nicholas's artwork. When she saw the mess in the back, she said she'd buy us all frankfurters and soda at the zoo.

After an hour at the zoo, Abby whispered to me, "We certainly are giving Nicholas an excellent introduction to the wonderful world of drinking fountains."

So far that's all Nicholas seems to be interested in. He stops at every drinking fountain and fools around with the knob. Then he tries to climb up. "Up, up, up," he says to one of us. But when we lift him up, he doesn't take a drink. He sticks his fingers over the nozzle and sprays everyone.

"Don't you want to see the animals?" Chuck asked him. Chuck loves to look at animals.

Nicholas nodded. "A-mals!" he said.

But, when we tried to show him the lion, he looked at everything in the cage *except* the lion.

He didn't seem to notice the elephant. But a

squirrel running across the lawn next to the frankfurter stand got him very excited. So did the pigeons around the trash cans.

Aunt Betsy got tired and sat down on a bench near the seals. Nicholas wasn't interested in the seals. He was busy getting chocolate ice cream all over his sailor blouse.

"Why don't you meet me back here in about an hour," Aunt Betsy said. "You can take Nicholas with you."

We were pleased she trusted us with Nicholas. "And there's still so much to show him," Will said as we started off.

Nicholas wasn't interested in tigers, monkeys, or giraffes.

"You know, Chuck," I said after a while, "I'm getting a little tired of watching Nicholas watch people take drinks from that water fountain." Chuck and I were sitting on a bench, waiting for Will and Abby. They had gone to get a plan of the zoo from the information center.

Abby came running toward us. Will was following behind her, studying a map of the zoo.

"We've got to see the polar bears," Abby called. "There's a new baby polar bear that's only five months old. Her name is Snow Puff!"

"Let's go." Chuck jumped to his feet.

"How would you like to see a nice polar bear?" Will asked Nicholas.

"Don't ask him," Chuck said. "Take him."

"But he's so interested in human behavior," Will said, pointing to the line of people waiting to get drinks of water.

I stooped down. "How about a nice piggyback ride?" I asked Nicholas.

Will gave me a look of disgust. "Don't you think Nicholas is beyond that sort of thing? Really, Toria!"

But Nicholas was already climbing up my back, dripping chocolate ice cream down my neck.

The polar bear exhibit is in a very natural setting. There is a curved stone wall low enough to see over, and a deep moat behind it which separates the people from the bears. There is no water in the moat. On the polar bear side there is a pool surrounded by rocks and caves.

There was a large crowd around the exhibit when we arrived, but slowly people began to move away. We found ourselves right up front. I lifted Nicholas up so he could see over the stone wall.

The mother bear, whose name is Iceberg, was fast asleep in the lazy afternoon sun. Only the front half of her was showing. The rest of her was inside a cave.

"Is that Snow Puff?" we heard someone in the crowd ask. "Over there—curled up next to her mother?"

"No, that's Iceberg's arm," someone else said. "Snow Puff must be fast asleep inside."

Will was standing next to me. "See the gweat big bear?" he asked Nicholas. "Gweat big furry white bear?"

Abby and I looked at each other. Will was talking baby talk!

Nicholas wasn't looking at the sleeping bear. He was looking up at the rocks on the opposite side.

"No, Nicholas," Will said. "Over there," and he pointed.

Nicholas kept looking the wrong way.

To my surprise, Will took Nicholas's head and twisted it so he could see the bear.

But Nicholas's eyes were still looking the wrong way.

"Nice doggie!" Nicholas shouted.

A few people around us laughed.

"Not a doggie," Will said. "A polar bear." He

read the sign on the wall out loud. " 'Polar bears are powerful swimmers. They are also very fast runners. Quite fearless, they will stalk and kill any animal, including man. . . .' "

"Nice doggie," Nicholas said. He pointed up the rocks on the other side.

I looked up and my heart sank.

There was a dog—a skinny white dog with black spots and long black floppy ears. He was carefully picking his way down the rocks.

"How did that dog get in there?" a woman behind me asked. "Dogs aren't allowed in the zoo."

"He must have gotten through that fence up there." Will pointed to the top of the rocks. "He's so skinny he might even have squeezed through the bars."

"I'm going to look for a zoo keeper right this minute," Chuck said and he took off.

"How long do polar bears sleep?" I asked Will.

The dog stopped at the polar bear pool. He lapped some water. Then he noticed the crowd staring at him over the stone wall. He walked around the pool and sat down right across the moat from where Nicholas and I were standing. He was looking right at Nicholas.

"Nice doggie," Nicholas whispered happily.

In no time at all Chuck was back with a zoo keeper. The zoo keeper stood next to me and stared at the black-and-white dog.

"What do you do in a situation like this?" a woman asked him.

"There has never been a situation like this," the zoo keeper said.

"Can't you go in there and save the dog?" a little girl asked him.

"We never go in that exhibit," the zoo keeper said. "Of all the animals at this zoo, those bears are the most dangerous. No one wants to get trapped with a polar bear. That's why we throw their food from behind that fence up there."

"Get out of there, you stupid mutt," a boy behind us yelled.

Abby whirled around and faced the boy. "Be quiet," she said angrily, "or you'll wake the bear!"

"No, no, no," the zoo keeper said. "The noise is good. The bears are used to certain noises— like the noise of the crowd. It could cover up any noise the dog might make."

Abby turned around again. "Make noise,"

she told the boy behind us. "Or you'll wake the bear."

"We have to *do* something," Chuck said.

The zoo keeper was very upset. He shook his head. "I'm afraid that little fella is just food for bears. Iceberg will polish him off!"

"Nice doggie," Nicholas said and he waved his chocolate ice-cream cone.

The dog sat there wagging his tail. Either he liked Nicholas's red hair or he was interested in the drippy ice-cream cone.

"Look," Will said, "things aren't too bad. We've got the first thing we need for any rescue."

"What's that?" Chuck asked.

"A channel of communication," Will said. "For some reason, Nicholas and that dog have something going on between them. Nicholas," Will said, "you are our Rescue Coordinator."

Nicholas turned and looked at Will. He looked back at the dog. Then he looked over at the sleeping bear. For a moment he looked quite serious.

"I think he understands," Abby whispered.

"Now, Toria, you hold Nicholas right there. Make sure the dog can always see Nicholas. If that dog panics, he's in trouble. If he tries to go back the way he came, he's finished."

"That's the truth," the zoo keeper said. "I'm surprised that bear isn't awake by now. Polar bears are usually very aware of anything strange in their territory. It's lucky for the dog the wind is blowing his scent away from Iceberg—but Iceberg might wake up any second now."

"Step two in a rescue," Will went on. "Tactics!" Will pronounced that word in a funny way. There were only three of us in that crowd who knew it was a signal. Will pronounced it, "T*A*C*K-tics!"

"Right," Chuck said quickly. "A bridge across the moat."

"A long board or something like that," Abby said. "That way no one has to go in, but the dog can escape across the moat."

"Not a bad idea," the zoo keeper said. "There might be some boards back at the shop but it will take me at least fifteen minutes to get there and back again."

"I'll go find some," Chuck said. A man in a safari jacket volunteered to go with Chuck. They went off to look.

Suddenly the whole crowd moaned, "Oh, no-o-o-o . . ."

Iceberg had stirred in her sleep. She rolled her head over to the other side.

The dog turned and looked. For the first time he saw he was not alone. He crouched down and started shivering. The hair all over his body seemed to stand up straight. He began creeping toward the edge of the moat.

Abby gasped. "I hope he doesn't try to jump!"

"He knows better than to jump," the zoo keeper said. "It's sixteen feet across that moat. He'll never make it. And it's thirty feet deep."

The dog was trembling.

"Toria," Will said, "tell Nicholas to say something reassuring to the dog."

There was no time to think of an easier word than reassuring. "Nicholas," I said, "say something *re-assur-ing* to the dog."

"What's the doggie's name?" Nicholas asked me.

"It's Spot," Abby said quickly.

"Good Spot," Nicholas called. Then he shook his finger at the sleeping bear.

"No more telebision," he told the bear.

It was an odd remark, but, for some reason,

the dog seemed to relax. He put his head down on his paws and looked sadly across the moat at Nicholas—as if Nicholas were his only hope.

"We've got some boards!" The crowd made way for Chuck and the man in the safari jacket. They were carrying two long wooden planks.

"We got them over by the construction site of the new House of Birds," Chuck explained.

The zoo keeper measured one of the boards. "Exactly sixteen feet," he said. "It won't reach across."

"But the moat is sixteen feet wide," Chuck said. "Oh, I see what you mean. The board has to be longer to reach from the stone wall to the edge of the ground where the dog is lying. It has to rest on something."

"But there are two boards," Abby said. "You can nail them together."

"Hammer and nails are back at the shop," the zoo keeper said.

"Can't someone lean out over the moat and hold the end of the board?" Chuck asked.

The zoo keeper shook his head. "Too difficult. Besides, it would be impossible to hold it steady. I don't think you can get a dog to walk across a shaky board. It's got to be solidly supported."

"We can tie the boards together!" Will said. He cupped his hands around his mouth and called out, "Does anyone here have anything like a rope or a strong belt?"

I looked around. People were shaking their heads. Everyone was wearing light summer clothes—shorts and shirts. No one seemed to be wearing a belt.

The polar bear stirred again. This time I was sure Iceberg was waking up! This time I had a feeling it was for real.

Will looked down at the two boards. He looked along the curved wall. The top was level with the ground the dog was standing on.

"We don't need to tie these together," Will said. "We can make a bridge!"

"They'll slip apart if you just put one on top of the other." The zoo keeper was horrified.

"No," Will said. "My idea is very simple."

Will made a bridge just in time. A few seconds later, Spot was safe. Can you guess how Will used those boards—before you turn this page?

Zoo T*A*C*K-tics

Will's Solution:

Will and Chuck lifted one board and placed it across the edge of the curved wall. They held it steady, while the zoo keeper and Abby slid the other board over the wall and the first board until it reached the other side of the moat. The two boards made a bridge shaped like a "T."

Nicholas called, "Here, Spot!" and Spot crossed the bridge just as Iceberg woke up and began to stretch.

Spot licked Nicholas's face and his ice-cream cone while the rest of us watched the mother and her baby polar bear play.

"Aren't those bears cute?" everyone said to everyone else.

"Now they seem cute." The zoo keeper laughed. He looked down at Nicholas and Spot. "Spot seems to have found a friend," he said.

Spot did have a friend. Nicholas had a wonderful time during his visit to Will's house.

When we went to say good-bye, Nicholas

picked up Spot's paw and waved to us.

Aunt Betsy sighed. "We went to the zoo and came home with a pet."

E–Z Parties, Inc.

Holly's birthday is next Saturday.

"I gave an invitation to every girl in my class," Holly said, "except Katrina."

"What?" my mother said. She was trying to park the car in front of Holly's ballet school. Holly and I were in the back seat.

"You have to invite Katrina." My mother turned off the car motor. "I gave you an invitation for every girl in your class. You can't leave one person out like that. It's cruel."

"You can't make me invite her." Holly folded her arms and slumped down in the seat. "Everyone hates her, and it's *my* party!"

My mother opened the car door without a word.

"Besides," Holly said sweetly, "I already tore up her invitation."

We dropped Holly off at her ballet class and went to the supermarket.

"Why does it have to be like this?" my mother asked me. "Why do I always have to suffer through Holly's birthday parties?"

My mother picked up a can of tuna, looked at the price, and put it back on the shelf.

"Last year Holly's party was an absolute nightmare," my mother went on. "Five minutes after the party started, there were already three little girls crying their eyes out. There were so many fights. Holly had a terrible time . . . and after all the work I did."

My mother sighed. She went back, picked up the tuna, and put the can into her shopping cart. "Maybe I'm just not very good at children's parties. I just wish someone would come along and take the whole thing off my hands— the plans, the party—everything!"

When we went to pick up Holly after her ballet lesson, she wasn't waiting in front of Madame Lyubova's Ballet School.

She was way down the block standing in front of a bakery window.

When she saw us, she called, "Quick, Mommy, Toria, come here. Come look at the birthday cake I'm getting. Hurry!"

"Holly!" my mother said when we reached the bakery. "You are *not* getting a cake from a bakery. It's much too expensive. I'm making your birthday cake."

Holly stamped her foot. "No," she said. "I want a store-bought cake. That's the only cake I want." Holly sighed. "Isn't it the most beautiful cake you ever saw?"

My mother and I looked at the cake. It was a tiny three-tiered white wedding cake with a bride and groom on the top.

"Don't be ridiculous!" My mother exploded. "That's a wedding cake. Look, Holly, I've had just about enough of your nonsense."

"But it's only twenty dollars!" Holly said. "I already asked."

My mother tried to talk in a reasonable tone. "Now, look. I was planning to spend twenty-five dollars for the entire party. Do you know how much it costs to get ice cream for twelve little girls?"

"We *have* to have ice cream," Holly said, and she climbed into the car.

"I can't stand it another minute," my mother whispered to me. We were still on the sidewalk. My mother was quiet for a moment.

"Toria," she said suddenly, "do you think you and Will would be interested in making a little money? I can't pay you much, but . . ."

Will was very excited when I called him.

"Just think, Toria," Will said, "if we do a good job of organizing Holly's birthday party, we can go into business. There must be parents all over Sandy Harbor suffering from children's birthday parties."

"We could call ourselves Parties, Incorporated," I suggested.

"What about Easy Parties, Inc.?" Will said. "You know, *E–Z*."

"That's a great name," I said, "but I'm afraid it's not going to be very E–Z. Can you come over? I have a few problems to discuss with you."

SUNDAY, SEPTEMBER 14—

"How in the world did you get Holly to invite Katrina?" my mother asked us. "And she did it so cheerfully!"

Holly had just called Katrina on the phone and told her that the cat had chewed up her invitation "by mistake."

"I just can't get over it!" my mother said. "Tell me how you did it."

"Oh, E–Z Parties has its ways," I told my mom. "Just relax and let E–Z Parties do the worrying."

Will and I looked at each other. E–Z Parties had plenty to worry about. We had just promised Holly that, if she invited Katrina, she would get the twenty-dollar wedding cake!

"Five dollars for the rest of the party?" Will and I were having a budget meeting. We were sitting in the hammock in my backyard. "We can't do it," Will said.

"Let's see," I said. "We have to have candles for the cake, and balloons, of course. Balloons are an absolute necessity. Besides, we can use them to decorate."

"We should get them all the same color," Will said. "That way they won't fight over them."

"Right." I wrote down "yellow balloons." "And we won't let those kids have the balloons till the end of the party. That way they can break their balloons on the way home and cry then."

Will said, "I guess we're doing pretty well. We have six good games that don't cost any money. Each lasts only fifteen minutes. Then twenty minutes for ice cream and cake. They'll be too busy to fight. No fighting, no crying."

"Oh, no!" I said.

"What's the matter, Toria?" Will asked.

"We forgot all about the ice cream," I told him. "We can't afford it!"

Holly came into the backyard. She stood by the back door holding a red ball.

"Listen," Will said to me. "I've got an idea."

Holly tiptoed over to us. "Are you talking about my party?" she asked shyly. "I promise I won't listen. Look. I'll play all the way over here." Holly kicked the ball away from us. "I can't hear a thing," Holly called.

She was only six feet away.

Will turned to me. "So anyway, Toria," he said, "as I was saying, that idea just won't work. Those kids just aren't mature enough. Let them have ice cream. Little kids like ice cream . . ."

Will glanced over at Holly. She had her back to us. She was holding very still, listening with all her might.

Will shook his head. "No, Toria," he said. "Those children are simply not grown-up enough for a dessert like (he lowered his voice) *Rainbow Mystery Delight.*"

I had no idea what Will was talking about, but I knew one thing: Rainbow Mystery Delight was a lot cheaper than ice cream.

Holly kicked the ball under the hammock— on purpose, of course. She had to crawl under us to fetch it.

"By the way," Holly said casually to Will, "did I ever tell you I don't really like ice cream. I hate it. I don't want any ice cream at my party. . . ."

FRIDAY AFTERNOON, SEPTEMBER 19—

"This has been the most relaxing week of my whole life," my mother said happily. "You two are doing a beautiful job!"

Will and I were in the kitchen making Rainbow Mystery Delight. It's a lot of work. You fill a glass with one color Jell-O, tilt the glass, and let it set. Then you add the next color and so forth until you have a rainbow . . .

"We'll be working all night," Will whispered to me.

"Can I help with anything?" my mother asked.

"Don't be silly," I said. "Why don't you just find a nice magazine and curl up on the couch."

HOLLY'S BIRTHDAY, SATURDAY, SEPTEMBER 20—

The backyard looks beautiful. Will and I hung yellow balloons from all the trees, and we put a yellow tablecloth on the picnic table.

I was setting the table with real china plates (paper plates cost too much), when I had a horrible thought.

"We have no prizes for the games!" I said. "Six games and no prizes!"

Will groaned. "There's thirty cents left in our party budget." Will flopped down on the hammock and stared up at the branches of an oak tree. "Six prizes for thirty cents! Impossible!"

Suddenly Will sat up. "Toria," he asked me, "are there any games that no one wins?"

I thought about it. "Well, yes," I said. "You know that game called Rumor where everyone sits in a circle? One person whispers a secret to the next one and they pass it along. It gets all mixed up. No one wins. It's just funny."

"Terrific!" Will shouted.

I felt very encouraged. "And what about a game where they all have to cooperate? Let's say they have to keep a balloon in the air . . ."

"With their noses!" Will said.

We thought of four games where no one wins. "Two to go," I said. "But I really hate to give up that Dress-Up Race. I worked so hard finding funny costumes for the two teams. But we have to have prizes for that one—six prizes!"

"Wait a minute," Will said. "I have an idea . . . it's never been done before, but . . ."

I could tell Will's mind was switching around. And it was switching fast!

"Leave it to me," Will said. "We'll have six prizes for thirty cents."

At that very moment I got an idea for another game. "And we can start with it!" I shouted.

THE START OF HOLLY'S BIRTHDAY PARTY, 2 P.M.

"But I have to meet my guests at the door," Holly said. "I have to collect my presents."

"You'll get them," I said. "We want you to wait until everyone's here. Then you can make a Grand Entrance."

"What's that?" Holly asked.

When I told her, she decided she would much rather make a Grand Entrance than greet her guests.

The little girls arrived. They were all dressed up. They all looked so cute and excited.

"Where's Holly?" they asked me.

"She's going to make a Grand Entrance," I told each little girl. "But first you have to hide your present in the backyard."

When Holly came down, everyone clapped. We took her into the yard and told her she had to search for her presents.

"Hey—wait a minute. What do I get if I find them?" she asked me.

"You get a present," I said.

"Oh, boy!" Holly shouted, and she raced off to look for her presents.

"That was a great idea for a substitute game," Will whispered to me.

"This is the best children's party I've ever been to," my mother whispered to me. "Everyone is having so much fun. There hasn't been a single fight!"

It was true. But now we were up to the Dress-Up Race. I felt a little nervous. How had

Will found six prizes for thirty cents?

Will explained the rules. Then he cleared his throat. "Now, the winning team gets the following prize. . . ."

All the little girls were staring up at him with big eyes.

"The winning team," Will said, "does *not* have to eat goblin eyes."

Holly's friends gasped and looked at each other.

"Goblin eyes?" a little girl named Gussie asked. "What are goblin eyes?"

"I don't think we're allowed to eat goblin eyes," her twin sister Samantha told Will.

But Will was already dividing up the teams.

The Dress-Up Race was a great success. When it was over, the losing team sat down in a circle on the grass, clutched each other's arms, and giggled.

"Help me blindfold them." Will handed me six strips of an old sheet.

I helped him put the blindfolds on the girls.

They were all shrieking. The winning team watched. They seemed a little jealous of the losers.

As it turned out, the losers had to eat peeled grapes.

"Blah!" they all said. "Goblin eyes. Blah!"

"Can we eat goblin eyes, too?" a girl on the winning team asked Will.

Will was surprised, but he said, "Of course," and went inside to peel six more grapes.

So everyone got to wear blindfolds, eat goblin eyes, and say, "Blah!"

The dessert was a great success. Everyone loved Rainbow Mystery Delight, and when Holly's wedding cake was delivered, everyone was very surprised—especially my mother.

"This is the best party I've ever been to," Katrina said. Everyone agreed.

"Let's have wedding cake at our birthday, too," Gussie said to her twin sister Samantha.

By the time every girl had a helping of cake, there was only one piece left.

Parents were beginning to arrive.

"Just a few more minutes to go," Will whispered.

"They've been so good!" my mother was saying to the other parents. They were all standing around by the back door. "Not a single fight. Holly is lucky to have such nice friends."

All of a sudden I heard Gussie say to Holly, "But you told me *I* could have the last piece."

"I want it," her twin sister Samantha said.

"Well, I didn't know you both wanted it," Holly said nervously. "You'll have to share."

Suddenly the air was filled with tension. All the other little girls looked up from their plates to see what was happening. The party became as quiet as the calm before a storm.

Gussie grabbed the cake knife. "I'll cut it," she said.

"No, I'll cut it," Samantha said. "She'll take the biggest piece."

"Toria will cut it," Holly announced. And she gave me a panicky look.

I picked up the cake knife and looked down at the little square of wedding cake lying on

the plate. I lifted the knife and looked at Will.

Will shrugged. "You cut better than I do, Toria."

"It won't be exactly even," I said.

"Then I get the biggest piece," Samantha said.

"No, you don't," Gussie said. "You had three goblin eyes and I only had one."

I just couldn't cut that cake! I heard murmurs from the other guests. The little girls were starting to take sides. There were three minutes left to the party and the place was about to explode in a big fight!

"Will," I whispered, "get me a ruler."

"It won't work, Toria," Will said. "First of all, that piece isn't an exact square. Secondly, one side is slightly higher than the other. You would have to do very complicated calculations to make it even."

"And a ruler will squish the icing," Holly added. "Hurry up, Toria. Cut it!"

My hand was trembling. I tried to line up the knife to make a diagonal cut.

"Wait a minute!" Will said. "I've got it. I know how to divide that piece of cake fairly."

"Will," I said, "you said there was no way to divide it evenly."

"Not divide it evenly," Will said. "Divide it *fairly!*"

"Nobody gets any?" I asked him.

Will shook his head. "No, they each get a piece."

With two minutes to go, Will told us his plan. There was no fight. Can you figure out what Will suggested—before you turn this page?

E–Z Parties, Inc.

Will's Solution:

Will said that one twin should cut the cake and the other would get to chose which piece she wanted.

Naturally, Gussie worked very hard to cut that piece even. Even so, she didn't do a very good job. One piece was bigger and her twin sister Samantha chose the bigger piece.

But then, to everyone's surprise, Samantha immediately gave Gussie a bite off her piece.

I heard a ripple of applause. I turned around. The grown-ups were applauding. They were all smiling, too!

Will and I got plenty of new business for E–Z Parties that afternoon.

"Don't I have nice friends?" Holly asked us afterward.

Halloween Shadows

"Halloween has lost its meaning," I said to Will. "It's not the least bit scary anymore. Just look at those kids."

A group of very small trick or treaters passed us. They were with their parents. They were all dressed up as television superheroes.

"Not a witch or a ghost in the bunch," I said. "And look at them digging into their candy before they even get home. All they think about is the food part! Where is the good old-fashioned terror? The spookiness? The slimy things grabbing at your ankles . . ."

"But it's still broad daylight, Toria." Will's voice was muffled behind his skeleton costume. "Halloween doesn't really start until it gets dark. After we finish taking Holly and Cyrus around, we'll go out by ourselves for some *serious* trick or treating. Wait until you see how my costume looks in the dark."

Holly and Cyrus were walking in front of us. This year Cyrus is Super-Mouse and Holly is a beautiful princess. She is wearing my mother's pink nightgown and a beautiful princess mask from the five-and-ten-cent store.

"The weather's all wrong, too," I went on. "It's so hot—just like summer. It isn't Halloween weather at all."

"Toria," Will mumbled through his costume, "I promise you. Halloween will get better later on."

"And then there's my costume," I said. "Isn't this the worst costume you ever saw? But I couldn't tell Mom that. She's been working on it for weeks. She wanted it to be a big surprise."

"I think it's very original," Will said. "I think it's a wonderful costume."

"It is not," I said. "It's not scary; it's not glamorous; it's hot; it's itchy; and I feel like a big fat lump in it."

"Come on, Toria," Will said. "I think a haystack costume is a great idea."

"I can hardly see through all this hay," I grumbled. "Why does my mom have to be so clever?"

We took Holly and Cyrus trick or treating along Main Street. Main Street is lined with elegant old houses. We stopped at the Pinkwater mansion first and Abby's grandmother gave us all ribbon candy. She didn't recognize any of us and I was pleased about that.

Then we went to the house next door. Mrs. Rae always gives us the same thing—frozen bite-sized Choc-O-Lishus bars.

When we got to the next house, Holly and Cyrus pulled back. They didn't want to go in.

"Mr. Woodrow always gives us healthy things," Holly said. "Those soy things and raisins."

"What's wrong with that?" I asked. "Mr. Woodrow doesn't believe children should eat candy."

"Children are supposed to eat candy," Holly said. "That's what children are for."

I looked up at Mr. Woodrow's house. Mr. Woodrow has no children. He lives all alone in a big house full of antiques and valuable paintings.

"Look, Will," I said. "He put a jack-o'-lantern in every window. He goes to so much trouble for Halloween. It makes me sad."

Will and I went up to the door and rang the bell. Holly and Cyrus followed us.

Mr. Woodrow opened the door right away.

"Well, well, well," he said. "This is your big night, isn't it?" We nodded and held our paper bags open for the treats.

Next came the estate of the Sweet family. It is an enormous white house with large columns in front. Judge Sweet is the richest man in Sandy Harbor.

This time *I* pulled back.

"Oh, come on, Toria," Will said in that muffled voice. "I'm sure what happened last year was an accident. Out of all those apples there's got to be one with a worm in it."

"It was the wrong kind of worm, Will," I said. "Joy Sweet gave me an apple with an earth-worm in it."

No one knows Joy or her older sister Bliss Sweet very well. They go away to boarding school. They are only around on weekends and holidays. But I never trusted them.

Holly and Cyrus didn't care about apples anyway, so we skipped the Sweet estate and continued down Main Street.

We didn't reach the last house until almost seven o'clock. Will and I promised our mothers we would get Cyrus and Holly home before dark.

"Time to go," I told Holly.

Holly protested. "But we haven't done the other side of Main Street yet."

"Don't worry," I said. "There's plenty in your bag to make you sick."

Will and I agreed to meet at eight o'clock across from the Pinkwater mansion and start on the other side.

"I'll see if Chuck can come," Will said. "Then we can bring our bags back to my house and eat our treats there."

Holly and I started home. We saw a little witch coming toward us, holding her father's hand.

"It's about time someone is wearing something scary," I said to Holly.

The witch suddenly stopped and clutched her father's arm. She pointed at Holly and began to scream, "What's that, Daddy? What's that?"

Now I must admit there is something grotesque about Holly's beautiful princess mask with its blond hair, glassy blue eyes, and smiling red lips, but I felt sorry for Holly.

"I'm beautiful," Holly said crossly to the witch as we passed by.

The little witch shrieked and hid her face in her father's sleeve. She began to sob, "Make it go away, Daddy. Make it go away."

"Dumb kid," Holly whispered. "She's scared of me."

I sighed. "Well, there's so little to be scared of nowadays, Holly. At least someone is feeling the true spirit of Halloween."

It was dark when I left the house again to meet Will. As soon as my mother closed the door, I crept around to the back of the garage and pulled an old sheet out of my treat bag. I took off my haystack costume, rolled it up, and stuffed it behind the woodpile. Then I took out Holly's little scissors and quickly cut two holes in the sheet for eyes.

I did it too quickly. The holes were too far apart, so I had to cut another hole between those two.

"Well, three eyes are even scarier," I told myself, and I put the sheet over my head. I picked up my bag of treats and ran down the driveway to the sidewalk.

Now that it was dark, everything seemed different. It was still very warm out, but it was windy. The sheet flapped around my legs. Under the streetlights the swaying branches of trees made shadows all over the sidewalk. As I walked along I found myself trying to walk in the patches of light.

A group of trick or treaters passed me. They were older kids. I didn't recognize any of them. I began to walk faster.

For no reason at all I began to think about things jumping out of the bushes at me. I ran the last few blocks to Main Street.

I was sorry I had done that. When I looked at my watch, I saw I was ten minutes early. Ten minutes to stand around and flap in the breeze. I looked up at the moon. It seemed to be racing across the sky in and out of the clouds. Ten minutes to look at that moon.

I was also sorry I had agreed to meet Will in
this particular place. Across from Abby's
grandmother's house is the Old Sailors' Church.
It is just a crumbling ruin set back from the
street in a clump of pine trees. In front of it is
an old graveyard that goes back to the early
days of Sandy Harbor. Most of the tombstones
are so worn, you can't even read the names on
them.

I found myself peering into the graveyard
just to make sure nothing was moving around.
I turned my back on the graveyard. That made
it worse.

Just when I had decided to go across the
street and ask Grandma Abigail for a drink of
water, I saw Will and Chuck. They were early,
too.

Will's costume looked great. The bones glowed
greenish white in the dark. Chuck was wearing

a ghost costume—just like mine.

Instead of crossing the street to meet me, they turned in at the gate to the Pinkwater mansion. A minute later they ran down the walk and went next door to Mrs. Rae's house. Next they went to Mr. Woodrow's . . .

I figured Chuck wanted to go to all the houses he had missed. I didn't care. It was still early. I sat down on the curb and waited. Carefully I spread my sheet out around me.

When I looked up again, Chuck and Will were running across the street toward me. I stood up. "We still have time," I said. "It's not even eight o'clock yet."

They stopped running and froze as if they had seen a ghost. Then they ran past me—into the graveyard.

"Hey!" I called. "Where are you two going?"

Then I realized that Will and Chuck were expecting to meet a haystack—not a ghost.

I ran after them into the graveyard. I caught a glimpse of some greenish white bones slipping behind a tombstone.

"Don't be scared," I called. "It's only me!"

Unfortunately, my voice echoed around and sounded like this: "IT'S O-O-ONLY ME-E-E. . . ."

Now I was sure I had scared them.

I walked over to the place I had seen the skeleton, but no one was there.

"It's me, Toria!" I called. "I changed my costume."

Out of the corner of my eye I saw a greenish glow and a flash of white near a big elm tree. I walked over to it and peeked around it.

"Don't be scared," I said to nobody at all.

I looked around. Nothing was moving except the leaves of the trees and the tall grass blowing in the wind. The clouds crossing the moon made shadows across the silent graveyard.

Then I thought I heard some whispering and a giggle.

All at once I was very sorry I had complained to Will that Halloween wasn't scary anymore.

"Very funny," I called. "You can come out now."

Silence.

"The joke's over," I called. "You proved your point, Will."

I waited. I felt a sharp tingle behind my left ear. I held very still. I felt that tingle again.

Now, I happen to be very sensitive about certain things. I knew I was being watched.

I turned around and looked up into the

branches of the elm tree. The skeleton and ghost were sitting up there, dangling their paper bags and looking at me.

My heart was pounding even though I knew who they were. I was scared, but I was angry, too.

"I'm going home now," I told them. "You can call me later and apologize."

I turned around and tried to walk out of the graveyard in a dignified manner. I had only gone a few steps when I ran into the skeleton again.

"Toria," the skeleton said. "What are you doing yelling around in here?"

"You know perfectly well what I'm doing, Will," I said angrily. "I'm chasing you and Chuck around."

"But I just got here." Will sounded puzzled. "Chuck couldn't come."

"Well, then, who's the ghost sitting with you up in that tree?" I pointed to the skeleton and ghost perched in the branches of the elm watching us silently.

I was so angry at Will it took me a few seconds to realize that what I had just said was ridiculous. I began to tremble.

"Will," I whispered to the bones standing

next to me, "are you sure it's really you?"

"Of course," Will said sharply.

"Then what, may I ask, is sitting in that tree?" I felt quite weak. "Why don't they talk?"

"Toria," Will said gently, "you probably scared them half to death. They're just kids dressed up in the same costumes as you and me."

That made sense. In fact, suddenly everything made sense. I had followed the wrong pair of trick or treaters into the graveyard.

Since everything made such perfectly good sense, it was hard to understand why Will was screaming.

I turned and stared at him. There were two large white flabby hands shaking him by the shoulders. It was quite an awful sight to see those glowing bones shaking around in the dark. Will's bag of treats dropped to the ground.

I don't know what made me so brave. I dropped my bag and rushed over to Will. I tried to get those awful hands off him. I grabbed them by the wrists and found myself struggling with Mr. Woodrow.

"Mr. Woodrow," I said. "I am surprised at you."

"*You're* surprised? What do you mean?" Mr. Woodrow's voice was high-pitched. He sounded hysterical. "How dare you throw ink in my window? I saw you do it. And after I had just given you your Halloween treats." He stopped shaking Will, but he still had a tight grip on Will's shoulders.

"So you caught them," a voice behind me said. I turned around and saw Mrs. Rae. She marched over to me and grabbed my arm. "I thought I saw them running around out here."

"But we didn't do anything," Will said.

"Don't lie," Mr. Woodrow said. "I saw you two at my house less than five minutes ago. I was sitting right in my living room when you reached in and threw the bottle of ink all over my Oriental rug. Believe me, it's going to cost your parents a fortune."

Mrs. Rae squeezed my arm. "And I don't think putting rotten eggs in my mailbox is very funny either, but at least you can clean it out. It's not ruined the way Mr. Woodrow's rug is ruined. You should be ashamed of yourselves." She pulled me by the arm. "Come on, we're calling your parents right this minute."

"Wait a minute," I said. "The kids who did it

are right there—right up in that tree." I pointed.

Mrs. Rae looked up at the skeleton and ghost in the tree. Mr. Woodrow looked, too. Then they both looked back at me and Will.

Mr. Woodrow let go of Will's arm. "There are two sets of them. Two sets of skeletons and ghosts." He sounded bewildered.

I looked at the skeleton and ghost in the tree. I was beginning to wonder if there were human beings inside those costumes when the ghost spoke:

"Oh, Mr. Woodrow," she whimpered, "I'm so glad you got here. They were scaring us so much."

"Is that you, Joy?" Mrs. Rae asked.

"Yes, Mrs. Rae," the ghost said politely. "It's me and my sister Bliss."

Mrs. Rae had tightened her hold on my arm. "It's Judge Sweet's little girls," she said to Mr. Woodrow.

Dragging Will by the arm, Mr. Woodrow went over to the tree and helped Joy and Bliss Sweet down.

The skeleton placed her bag carefully on the ground and dusted herself off. "We were on our way home when we saw those two running out of Mr. Woodrow's house," Bliss said, pointing to me and Will. "Then they came after us and tried to grab our bags of treats." Her voice was shaky.

I was so angry I was speechless.

"I believe you, dear," Mrs. Rae told Bliss. "Don't be frightened." Then she said to Mr. Woodrow. "They're *such* nice girls."

"We're nice, too!" I yelled. "The skeleton you're dragging around happens to be Will Roberts and I'm Toria Gardner!"

With that, I pulled the sheet off my head. I thought it was pretty dramatic.

Mrs. Rae said, "Toria Gardner! I am surprised at you for doing such a thing!"

"Will Roberts, too," Mr. Woodrow said. "You were such a nice youngster. What happened?"

"But we didn't do it," Will said. "We haven't been to your house in the last two hours."

"That's right!" I shouted. "And I can prove it!"

"Go right ahead," Mr. Woodrow said.

"Well," I began, "you see, I'm not really a ghost. About six o'clock, if you'll remember, a skeleton, a beautiful princess, a Super-Mouse, and a haystack came to your house—right?"

"A hundred kids came to my house," Mr.

Woodrow said. "But, as a matter of fact, I do remember a bundle of straw."

"Well, that was me," I said. "That proves I was there at that time."

I thought I heard Will groan.

"That proves," Mrs. Rae said impatiently, "that you changed your costume, came back, collected your treats a second time, put rotten eggs in my mailbox, and destroyed Mr. Woodrow's precious Oriental rug."

"No," I said, "Joy and Bliss Sweet were the ones who were just there. I saw them." I had another idea. "And I can prove it!"

I held up my sheet for them to see. "Look at this sheet," I said. "If you'll notice, it has three eyes in it. The ghost over there—Joy Sweet—has two eyes. The ghost who was at your houses a few minutes ago had two eyes—correct?"

"Young lady," Mrs. Rae said, "we have better things to do than count eyes on ghosts."

Suddenly I was desperate. "Well, then," I said, "what about the earthworm?"

"The *what*?" Mr. Woodrow stared at me.

"Toria," Will said quietly, "I wouldn't dig up that earthworm right now. I don't think it will help us."

"But don't you see, Will?" I said. "It will prove what nasty little sneaks those Sweet sisters are."

"I don't know about you, Mr. Woodrow," Mrs. Rae said, "but I've had quite enough of this nonsense."

"Will," I said, "think of some proof. Think, Will, think."

"Thinking won't help," Will said flatly.

"Well, then, tell them. Tell them we didn't do it!" I wanted to strangle Will.

"Telling won't help either," Will said. "Don't you see? They've already made up their minds that we did it. We've got to see it from their side."

"What?" I asked Will.

"Look, Toria." Will sounded defeated. "There's a pretty good case against us. We might as well just go over what happened—step by step."

I couldn't believe Will was saying this!

"Let's say Toria and I did it . . ." Will began.

"Well, it's about time you admitted it," Mrs. Rae said.

My mouth fell open.

"About five minutes ago," Will went on, "a ghost and a skeleton came to your door, Mrs. Rae, and you gave us each a frozen chocolate bar. Neither of us spoke. We didn't even say 'thank you.' "

"No, you did not," Mrs. Rae said stiffly.

"Right," Will said. "And after you closed the door, we put rotten eggs in your mailbox, went next door, and got raisins and soy things from Mr. Woodrow. Then we ran back and threw a bottle of ink into his living room window."

Mrs. Rae and Mr. Woodrow began to relax. They were nodding their heads. Finally they were getting the truth!

Joy and Bliss were looking at each other.

They must be surprised, I thought, hearing Will confess like that. I certainly was!

Crazy thoughts went through my head. I kept thinking of the look on my mother's face when she found out I was no longer a haystack.

"Can we go now?" Joy Sweet asked Mrs. Rae. "Our parents will be getting worried about us."

"Of course, dear," Mrs. Rae said. "I'm just sorry these two went and spoiled your Halloween. They spoiled everyone else's Halloween, too. Now run along and enjoy your treats."

"We're sorry we spoiled your Halloween," Will said to Bliss and Joy. "But, before you go, would you mind showing us what's in your bag. It will only take a second."

"Aha!" I said. "Traces of ink. Rotten egg shells."

"No, Toria," Will said. "Something quite harmless."

Bliss Sweet shrugged her skeleton costume. "We'll show you what's in our bags. We don't mind."

"Good," Will said.

My head was spinning. Bliss and Joy were guilty—beyond the shadow of a doubt. Do you know what gave them away? Try to figure it out before you turn the page.

Halloween Shadows

Will's Solution:

Joy and Bliss each had the frozen Choc-O-Lishus bar Mrs. Rae had just given them. Of course, theirs were still cold and hard, with drops of moisture forming on them.

We had gotten our chocolate bars hours before, so they were quite soft and mushy.

Mr. Woodrow and Mrs. Rae were horrified.

"I think it's time to have a nice long chat with Judge Sweet," Mrs. Rae said.

After they'd all gone, I turned on Will.

"Will Roberts, you scared the life out of me—confessing like that!"

Will leaned down and picked up his bag of treats.

"I took a risk," Will admitted. "But I needed time to go over what had happened. I had a feeling something would turn up."

"But, Will," I said, "what if . . ."

The moon went behind the clouds and stayed there. The graveyard was now pitch dark.

"Toria," Will said, "do you mind if we continue this discussion elsewhere?"